Disney · PIXAR
BRAVE
TAKE AIM!

By Mona Miller
Illustrated by the Disney Storybook Artists

Random House New York

Copyright © 2012 Disney/Pixar. All rights reserved. Published in the United States by Random House Children's Books, a division of Random House, Inc., 1745 Broadway, New York, NY 10019, and in Canada by Random House of Canada Limited, Toronto. Random House and the colophon are registered trademarks of Random House, Inc.
ISBN: 978-0-7364-2967-2
randomhouse.com/kids
MANUFACTURED IN CHINA
10 9 8 7 6 5 4 3 2 1

3-D special effects and production: Red Bird Publishing Ltd., U.K.

MERIDA

Redheaded Merida is the Princess of the kingdom of DunBroch in the mysterious Highlands of Scotland. Though she has many duties, she would much rather be out exploring and shooting her bow and arrow.

"Every once in a while, there's a day when I don't have to be a princess. No lessons and no expectations!" Merida says about her chances to enjoy freedom in the outdoors.

ANGUS

Merida loves riding her horse, Angus,
over the hills and through the countryside.
The cautious Clydesdale
keeps his eye on
Merida, whose
love of adventure
sometimes leads
them both
into trouble.

Angus always listens to Merida—and he's always ready for a good gallop through the forest.

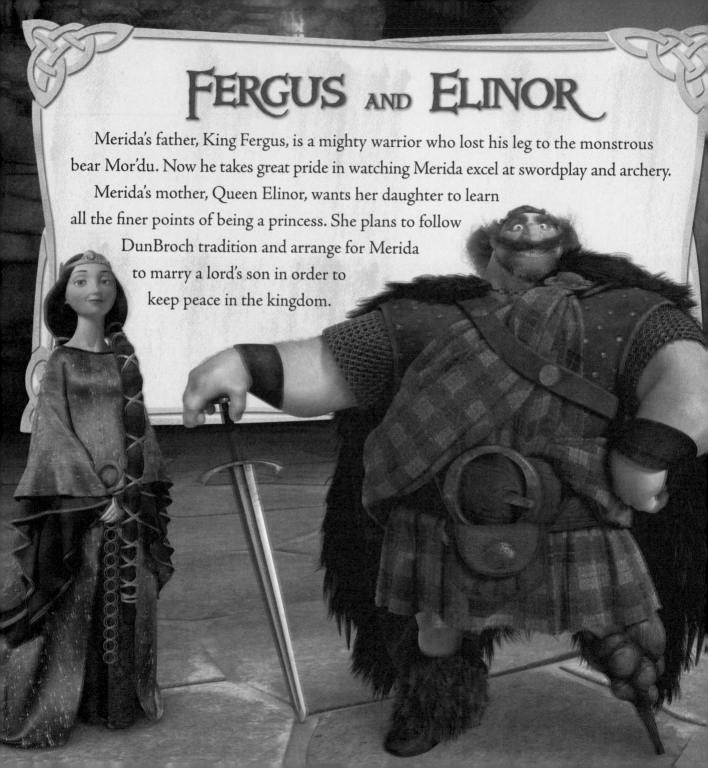

FERGUS AND ELINOR

Merida's father, King Fergus, is a mighty warrior who lost his leg to the monstrous bear Mor'du. Now he takes great pride in watching Merida excel at swordplay and archery. Merida's mother, Queen Elinor, wants her daughter to learn all the finer points of being a princess. She plans to follow DunBroch tradition and arrange for Merida to marry a lord's son in order to keep peace in the kingdom.

Fergus, who loves sword fighting and archery as much as Merida does, often takes his daughter's side and good-naturedly tells Elinor, "Och! Leave her be!"

THE LORDS' SONS

Queen Elinor arranges for a contest among the neighboring clans in which the eldest sons of three lords compete to marry Merida. Soon the lords arrive for the Highland Games and present their sons: Young Macintosh, Wee Dingwall, and Young MacGuffin. Each lord hopes his son will win the Games—and win Merida's hand.

"Well done, lad! That's my boy!" Lord Dingwall cries—even though Wee Dingwall
has hit the bull's-eye in the archery competition completely by accident.

WILL O' THE WISPS

After a fight with her mother, Merida races into the forest to escape the responsibilities of being a princess. At the mysterious Ring of Stones, she follows some small blue flames called the will o' the wisps deeper into the dark woods. Legend holds that these blue flames can lead the way to a new fate.

Merida follows the wisps to a wood-carver's cottage. There, she discovers a reluctant witch who cooks a magical cake for her. The princess takes the cake home and hopes it will solve all her problems.

ELINOR-BEAR

When Queen Elinor eats the enchanted cake, Merida's plan to change her mother works. Unfortunately, it isn't Elinor's mind that changes—she transforms into a big, black bear! Merida must find a way to undo the spell and protect the queen from King Fergus, who hasn't looked too kindly on bears ever since Mor'du bit off his leg.

Even as a bear, Elinor reacts quickly when her daughter falls through the floorboards of an ancient castle—and into the clutches of Mor'du!

HARRIS, HUBERT, AND HAMISH

Merida's little brothers are identical triplets who love to get in trouble and eat anything sweet. The triplets get both when they nibble on the leftover enchanted cake and turn into bear cubs!

The cub triplets quickly realize that Merida still knows who they are.
When the time comes, they race to their sister's rescue!

When Merida says, "No matter what you are, you're my mother," the spell is finally broken! Elinor and the triplets return to their human forms. Fergus and Elinor agree that Merida should marry only when she chooses to. With all well in the kingdom, Merida takes aim at a bright new future—and a fate of her own making!